IVOR

the engine
The Elephant

Story by OLIVER POSTGATE
Pictures by PETER FIRMIN

The evening sun lit each puff of steam
that rose from the funnel of Ivor the Engine
as he trundled peacefully homeward pulling
a flat truck with a basket of pigeons on it.

Leaning out of his cab watching the warm
sunlit landscape roll past, were Jones the
Steam who was Ivor's driver and Evan Evans,
who was known as Evans the Song because
he was choirmaster of the Grumbly and District
Choral Society.

With Ivor's help they had persuaded the
twenty-eight pigeons to fly down off the
roof of Miss Price's little house at Llangubbin
and settle in the basket. Now they were
taking them home to Mr Brangwyn.

Very calm and contented they felt as they
listened to the quiet thudding of Ivor's
pistons and the clip-clop of the rails under
his wheels.

PSSSTWHOOP . . . PSSST ZONK!
Ivor had slammed on his brakes!

Jones and Evans piled up in the cab and the truck and pigeons nearly lifted off the rails.

"Yowch!" wailed Jones, rubbing a badly bumped nose.

He climbed down and spoke sternly.

"Now look here, Ivor, you know as well as I do, you are not supposed to slam on your brakes like that!"

"Excuse me," said Evans, "I think perhaps Ivor was right to stop."

"Indeed?" said Jones, with dignity.

"Well, yes, there is a rock on the line."

There was something on the line.

Something large and lumpy and grey.

Jones the Steam inspected it.

"That's not rock!" he announced, "that's elephant!"

"Oh, so it is! A dead elephant!"

"Not dead, just resting," said Jones. "Come along now, Elephant! Time to wake up!"

The elephant opened an eye.

"Sorry. to disturb you and that, but this is a railway line, you see."

The elephant understood. It sighed and slowly began to move. After much rolling and heaving it was on its feet. Then it began to walk away.

The elephant's walk was unsteady.

"Oh look!" cried Evans. "It has a bad foot! What shall we do?"

"Well there's only one thing we can do, isn't there?" replied Jones.

So they did it.

They ran after the elephant and invited
it to wait for them.

They took the basket of pigeons off the
truck and persuaded the elephant to sit in
its place. Then they tied the box of pigeons
very carefully on top of the elephant.

"Now you hold tight on the corners,
Elephant bach," said Jones, "we don't want
you rolling off."

POOOP . . . CHUFF CHUFF CHUFF . . .

"That's all very well," said Evans the Song, "we've got the elephant on to the truck but where are we taking it?"

"Oh well, we shall have to think about that," said Jones the Steam.

They thought. They tried to think of somebody who had room enough and time enough and kindness enough to look after a wounded elephant.

Then, with one voice, they shouted: "Mr Hughes the Gasworks!"

They took the elephant to the gasworks
but Mr Hughes the manager was a bit reluctant
to receive an elephant as a guest.

"But you're known to be a great animal
lover, Mr Hughes!" cried Jones.

"Budgerigars, Mr Jones! It's budgerigars
I keep, not elephants!"

"Oh look!" sighed Evan Evans, "the poor
thing is shivering! It's cold!"

Jones and Evans stood and waited. They
knew that was all they had to do.

In the end Mr Hughes gave an angry snort.
"Oh all right then! I'm the idiot as
usual!" he shouted, "get it unloaded and
dump it over there!"

Once he had decided to accept his huge
guest, Mr Hughes could not have made it
more welcome. He fetched straw and canvas
for a bed. He built a tarpaulin tent to
keep off the wind. He even fitted up a

special gas fire for the elephant's personal comfort.

"Well, what's the point of living in the gasworks if you can't keep warm?"

The elephant ate nine loaves of stale bread kindly given by the baker, drank a bucket of water and then settled gratefully down on the bed, closed its eyes, sighed and slept.

The next day Miss Ludgrove the vet came by to examine the elephant.

"Ah, she's a very healthy-looking young thing," said Miss Ludgrove. "Can you get her to sit up while I look at her foot and listen to her chest?"

Jones asked the elephant to sit up. She not only sat up, she held up her foot for inspection.

"Oh you're good with elephants, Mr Jones. Can you ask her to say ninety-nine?"

"Oh don't be daft, Miss Ludgrove!"

"Yes, she has a nasty cut on that foot.
You must bathe it in hot water and disinfectant,
hot water, mind, as hot as she can stand.
Oh yes, and administer sixteen of these
horse pills every four hours."

Miss Ludgrove departed.

"Er, Jones," said Evans, "are you going
to administer the pills?"

"Certainly," said Jones the Steam.
"How?"

They tried different ways. They offered
her the pills on a plate. She blew them
across the yard.

They hid them in some bread but she
wouldn't eat the bread.

They hid them in cabbage leaves but she
just shook them out.

In the end Jones fetched a cardboard tube
and tried to blow them into her mouth.

The elephant blew first!

That was no good, so they decided to
bathe her foot.

Kettles of boiling water, a bottle of disinfectant, a huge tin bath, a big old curtain for a towel, everything they needed was fetched.

Jones prepared the bath and set it beside the elephant.

"Come along now, Elephant bach, lift up your bad foot and put it in the nice warm bath. Come along, it will do you good."

There is no doubt Jones was good with elephants. The elephant lifted her foot and placed it gently into the steaming bath.

"There now," said Jones.

"EEEEEEOWOOOOOW!" screeched the elephant.

SPLODGE SLURP CLUNK BINGBANG BONK PLOOF.

That was the bath, the water, the towel,
the disinfectant, Evans the Song and Jones
the Steam all falling about in different
directions as the elephant lashed out.

"Oh that'll do!" shouted Jones the Steam,
"I've had enough of elephants! Let's go and
take Mr. Brangwyn his perishable pigeons!"

POOOP . . . CHUFF CHUFF CHUFF . . .

"HO HO HO HO HO HO!" How Mr Brangwyn
laughed when he heard what had happened!
"What a carry-on! HO HO HO! Nursing an
elephant now is it? That's a skilled job,
I know! I lived in India . . ."

Suddenly Mr Brangwyn stopped laughing.

"I've got just what you want!" he said.

He dashed indoors and fetched an object.
A strange thing it was, like a leather
bucket with laces.

"Here you are," he said, "I bought it in

Bangalore forty years ago."

"Oh yes," said Jones, "very nice. But what is it?"

"Elephant's boot, man! Elephant's boot!" roared Mr Brangwyn. "You bandage the foot and put on the boot. Take it! I don't need it!"

"Oh, right-ho then, thank you."

They tied the boot on to the flat truck and set off back to Grumbly.

POOOP . . . CHUFF CHUFF CHUFF . . .

"Oh my goodness! Oh my golly gosh!"

As Ivor passed the place where they met the elephant a dark man leaped over the hedge and ran after them.

"Oh dear me! Please wait! Wait for me!"

He ran down the railway, shouting and waving his arms.

"Hey Jones," said Evans, "somebody is chasing us. Funny-looking bloke! Wearing a pudding-cloth on his head!"

"Stop, Ivor!"

PSSSST CLOP.

"Oh my goodness gracious!" panted the dark man. "Oh you are kind to stop. Oh, oh, I am Bani Moukerjee and I wish to ask you one question. Why do you carry an elephant's boot? Is it for my Alice?"

"Is your Alice an elephant?"

"Oh yes! She is lost and I am in such trouble if I do not find her!"

"Well, I reckon you do find her," said Jones the Steam. "Jump on and we'll be down there in a jiffy."

POOP . . . CHUFF CHUFF CHUFF . . .

When Alice saw Bani she lifted her trunk and trumpeted.

"WHEEEEOWP!"

Bani ran to embrace her.

"Oh you are bad! Oh Alice you are bad!"

He wept and held her tight.

"Oh Alice, what would I have done if I had not found you? Oh Alice, you are bad! bad! bad!"

Bani beat her thick hide with his fists and wept for joy.

"Oh I thank you for caring for my Alice. Now she is safe and well and all right!"

"Well, not quite all right," said Jones, "She has a badly cut foot."

"Alice is hurt?" said Bani, serious at once. "Show me!"

Alice lifted her foot.

"That has to be bathed in very hot water and disinfectant twice a day and sixteen of these horse-pills every four hours."

"Oh, thank you most kindly," said Bani.

He took the box of pills. "Now Alice, open
the mouth very widely please!"

Alice opened her mouth.

Clop, clop, clop, clop, clop, clop, clop, clop,
clop, clop, clop, clop, clop, clop, clop, clop.

Bani threw in the sixteen horse-pills.

"Now close your mouth and chew!"

Alice closed her mouth and chewed.

"Now please to swallow!"

Alice made a terrible face but she did
as she was told, she swallowed the pills.

"Oh you are a good elephant," cried Bani. "Oh you are good and beautiful!"

Then they prepared to bathe her foot.

When the time came for her to put her foot in the bath Jones and Evans took cover behind the tent.

Alice gave a very small squeak as she put her foot in the water but that was all.

"She has done it!" shouted Jones.

"But of course," replied Bani.

"Oh dear! You should have seen the mess

when we tried! Water everywhere! Pills all over the yard!"

"Alice was disobedient?" cried Bani, "Oh Alice, you are badder and badder! Say you are sorry!"

Alice knelt with her forehead on the floor and squeaked.

"Oh, get up now, Elephant bach," said Jones, "we know you didn't mean any harm. Hold still while I dry your foot!"

They dried and bandaged Alice's foot and put on the boot.

"Oh it is fitting!" cried Bani, "Oh you
are kind and good! Now I can sit down. Three
days I have been sitting down not at all,
searching for my Alice!"

Bani settled on the canvas by Alice. He
took out a little pipe and began to play
a lullaby.

Jones and Evans crept away.

Soon the pipe fell from Bani's fingers
and he slept, safe with his elephant by their
own gas fire in Grumbly Gasworks.

The next morning they were up early.

Alice stood on a pile of coal, looking out over the wall and listening with her huge ears.

"She is hearing something," said Bani.

"WEEEEOWP!" trumpeted Alice.

Faintly, from far away, came an answering call.

"Oh Alice! Lift me up!"

Alice lifted Bani lightly on to her back.

"Oh yes, they are coming! All my elephants are coming!"

"All of them?" asked Jones.

"Yes and the lions and the seals and the Lady with the Snakes and the high-wire and the funny-men. They are Mister Charlie Banger's Circus and they are coming here!"

Bani was quite right. Soon a colourful cavalcade of lorries and cages drew into the quiet square of Grumbly Town.

"Excuse me!" shouted Charlie Banger, "does anybody happen to have seen an elephant?"

"What colour elephant?" asked Mr Rees.
"WHEEEOWP!"
"There she is!"
What a thundering and trumpeting there was in Grumbly as Alice ran to greet the other elephants!
When Charlie Banger heard how kind everybody had been to his elephant he insisted on showing his appreciation with a free show for everybody in the town.

"Roll up! Roll up! Free show tonight!
Everybody invited! Be Charlie Banger's guests!"
Oh the excitement!
Ivor rushed back to Llaniog, collected
everybody he could find in any trucks and
carriages and sped back to Grumbly.
Boom Boom Tarara Boom-boom!
Boom Tiddley-om pom POM! POM! POM!
the band was playing and the big tent filled
the square as Ivor drew in.

Oh, what a marvellous circus that was!
Plumed ponies pranced and light-footed
ladies danced from one to the other. A man
rode a one-wheel cycle on a wire. A golden
cage of gentle lions had a fierce man in it.
He was The Great Galvani!
There were seals and funny-men and a lady
with snakes, but best of all were the elephants
and best of all the elephants was Alice,
all dressed up in gold and glitter.

Jones and Evans clapped until their hands were sore and then, when it was all over, Charlie Banger and his friends came and sat around Ivor's boiler and had a cup of tea.

This edition published 1994 by Diamond Books
77-85 Fulham Palace Road, Hammersmith London W6 8JB

First published by Picture Lions 1979
14 St James's Place, London SW1

Printed in Slovenia

ISBN 0 261 66572-3